William Kemp

Obstetrical Notes, based on 1,000 Cases of Delivery

Anatiposi

William Kemp

Obstetrical Notes, based on 1,000 Cases of Delivery

Reprint of the original.

1st Edition 2023 | ISBN: 978-3-38230-150-7

Anatiposi Verlag is an imprint of Outlook Verlagsgesellschaft mbH.

Verlag (Publisher): Outlook Verlag GmbH, Zeilweg 44, 60439 Frankfurt, Deutschland
Vertretungsberechtigt (Authorized to represent): E. Roepke, Zeilweg 44, 60439 Frankfurt, Deutschland
Druck (Print): Books on Demand GmbH, In de Tarpen 42, 22848 Norderstedt, Deutschland

OBSTETRICAL NOTES,

BASED ON

1,000 Cases of Delivery.

Read at the Annual Session of " The Medical and Chirurgical Faculty of Maryland,"
in June, 1859, as the Report of the Committee on Obstetrics.

By WILLIAM KEMP, M.D.,

OF BALTIMORE, MARYLAND.

[From the American Medical Monthly for July, 1859.]

We propose to analyze the first one thousand cases of delivery that occurred in our experience, and to offer such thoughts and comments as may be deemed appropriate, under the respective heads which usually include the facts of midwifery statistics. We have taken the first thousand cases as they are registered, and limit the analysis to them, for want of time to consider the entire register, in readiness for the meeting of the Faculty.

The condensed character necessary for a report, precludes enlargement upon several topics of momentous importance, which it behooves the accoucheur to understand, and with which he is morally bound to acquaint himself, so as to be furnished for emergencies, or for prompt action, where delay or want of information may entail an unnecessary degree of suffering or mental anxiety on the parturient patient. We shall present the subject as it relates,

    1st. To the mother.
    2d. To the child.

1

PERTAINING TO THE MOTHER.

1st. *Whole Number of Children.*—The 1,000 cases of delivery produced 1,019 children; nineteen of the cases having borne twins.

2nd. *Age of the Mother when Delivered.*—I have not preserved a record of the ages of the mother in a sufficient number of cases to make the exhibit of any interest or value. The extremes of the ages, however, are accurately stated at 15 years and 43 years.

3rd. *Number of Times the Mothers had been Pregnant.*

Pregnancies	1	2	3	4	5	6	7	8	9	10	11	12	13
Mothers	213	165	130	84	48	30	12	12	3	5	2	5	1

It will be perceived that only 710 pregnancies are noted. There is difficulty in obtaining absolutely accurate numbers, in many cases, growing out of intercurrent abortions and miscarriages. The preceding table furnishes the following proportions in a thousand labors. The table is to be read thus: in every thousand cases, 300 will be first pregnancies, &c.

PROPORTION OF DIFFERENT PREGNANCIES IN 1,000.

Pregnancies	1	2	3	4	5	6	7	8	9	10	11	12	13
Proportion	300	232†	183†	118†	67†	42†	16†	16†	4†	7†	2†	6†	1†

4th. *Duration of Labor.*—I shall not offer any table of the duration of the labor. The difficulties which frequently embarrass the determining of the commencement of actual labor-pains, and the different phenomena which are regarded by different observers as constituting the commencement of labor, must give great uncertainty to the value of any such table, unless it be accompanied by lengthy notes and explanations. These would swell the present paper to an unjustifiable size. The recurrence of pains, with short intermissions, is usually regarded as diagnostic of incipient labor. This cannot be a fundamental truth. Women are frequently sorely distressed by pains of an intermittent character, accompanied by hardening of the uterus and tension of abdominal walls, imparting to them a sensation similar to the initial pains of former labors; and yet these pains may not be provoked by the cause of labor, but be dependent upon some trouble in the alimentary canal, or disorder in some other organ. I do not regard pain, *per se*, even of an intermittent character, as an indication that labor has commenced.

The commencement of labor should be acknowledged only when the pains are discovered to have a certain bearing on the os uteri, and on the uterine contents. The pains which constitute the commencement of labor will almost always be found to produce the same effects, and these effects will generally be in the same order of sequence. Upon *touching*, the following phenomena will be discovered if labor has really begun: Upon the incursion of pain, the margin of the os uteri becomes more rigid; the presenting part of the fœtus recedes from the finger; a greater or less quantity of amniotic water depresses the membrane within the os; and when the pain reaches its acme, the presenting part of the fœtus will again be brought down to the os uteri.

Although occasional cases occur in which the preceding circumstances obtain, and labor does not follow promptly, they must nevertheless be regarded as exceptional, and detract but little from the value which justly attaches to the signs as indices of imminent accouchement.

In an elaborate argument upon the order in which different portions of the uterus act in parturient pain, Wigand furnishes an account of the phenomena which constitute genuine pain. It is only pain characterized by these peculiarities which should be regarded as the commencement of labor. Ramsbotham says emphatically that "the presence of pain, even if it be periodical, is not always symptomatic of labor having begun."

The presence of a considerable quantity of vaginal fluid is not necessarily indicative of the commencement of labor.

Again, I am satisfied that tables of the duration of labor will exhibit different results, corresponding to the practical views entertained by the practitioners, who respectively tabulate the results of their experience, and that the value of such tables can only be estimated when the peculiar precepts which govern the practice are clearly stated.

There are two great classes of obstetricians, between whom the views entertained as to the manner of conducting a labor, form a line of distinction marked and emphatic. The comparative duration of labor, as experienced by these two classes of accoucheurs, in an extended series of cases, would be considerably discrepant, from the very principles by which the procedures of the two would be regulated. These two classes may be designated thus:

1st. Those who believe that a labor, in which the presentation is normal, and the position of the presentation is favorable to unassisted delivery, should be permitted to pass through its stages without interference on the part of the accoucheur, *provided no symptoms involving the life or physical safety of the patient arise.* The probable duration of the labor and the possible evils to result from it are not allowed to weigh against the emphatic precept, " A meddlesome midwifery is bad." The great precept with this class is, to wait patiently for the processes of nature.

2nd. Those who inculcate the necessity for a steady exercise of patience in simple cases, but who nevertheless are convinced that it must be exercised with a limitation. They hold, that oftentimes the stages of a labor may be abridged by judicious assistance; that the accoucheur is morally bound to study the indications for, and the manner of, rendering this assistance; and that the parturient woman is entitled to, and of right ought to have, such assistance judiciously and opportunely administered.

In the ranks of the former class we find the names of those who are high authority in midwifery, and who have exercised a swaying influence over the professional mind of this country. In the front of these is Blundell, made so conspicuous among them by his boldly and often carefully repeating the aphorism, " A meddlesome midwifery is bad." Not the first in order of time, he is perhaps the most emphatic on this point.

Denman, in his instructions for the conduct of a labor, says, " he (the accoucheur) can do nothing until the womb dilates to admit the passage of the infant." Quotations from authors inculcating these views might be greatly multiplied, but the necessary limits of this paper preclude a more extended reference here.

In opposition to these views we have the dogma of Hamilton, that " the termination of the *first stage* of labor *should be secured* within twelve or fourteen hours from its actual commencement;" and his unequivocal assertion to support it, that " no patient under his charge for twenty-five years, has been above twenty-four hours in labor; and except in cases of disproportion, none so long." Not less decided is Burns, " that if a long time is spent in accomplishing the first stage of labor or dilatation of the os uteri, the vigor of the uterus and strength of the patient may be impaired so much as to render the subsequent stage dangerously tedious, or to prevent its completion, at least, consistently with safety. *The first stage of labor ought always to be accomplished within a certain time,* varying somewhat according to the constitution of the patient and the degree of pain. If the pains be continuing without suspension, or an interval of some hours, and the labor be going on all the time, but slowly, *it is a good general rule to effect the dilatation of the os uteri within ten or twelve hours*, at the farthest, from the commencement of labor." (James Burns, edit. 1839, pp. 309–310.) Professor Miller, of Kentucky, a very profound thinker and philosophical actor in obstetrics, is perhaps the strongest American advocate for the propriety and importance of these rules of practice. After an interesting consideration of the subject, and a tolerably full *résumé* of the question, he adds: " I have for many years been in the habit of employing them under the circumstances which have been pointed out in a great number of cases, and no evil consequences whatever have resulted, but labor has been greatly assisted, and many accidents, as I am firmly persuaded, have been averted. My testimony, founded on experience, is, therefore, in favor of the safety and efficiency of the practice." (*Human Parturition*, 1849, p. 150.)

To pursue this subject further would occupy too much space in a paper like the present, although it merits the most considerate attention. A thorough acquaintance with its practical details will enable the accoucheur to abridge, by hours sometimes, the suspense and suffering of the parturient woman.

5. *Flooding.*—I cannot give an accurate account of all the cases attended by hæmorrhage. Those which were unattended by any particular interest in the circumstances or treatment, were merely indicated without any detail. It would not be proper to rely upon memory to supply the particulars. The memoranda of some cases have been made with care, and it may not be uninteresting to advert to a few.

Flooding before Six Months.—A lady who was delivered on January 6th, 1844, was attacked by copious hæmorrhage on the preceding 27th of August. Notwithstanding its arrest by perfect quietude, cool local applications, and internal means, it recurred frequently without any apparent provoking cause, and unattended by any pains of labor. Her strength finally became greatly reduced, and her general condition anæmic. The plan of treatment was essentially altered, and directed mainly to the reinvigoration of vital forces. She was taken from her house in a carriage properly prepared, and sent by steamboat on excursions on the Chesapeake Bay, to receive the impression of mental gratification and bodily exposure to air impregnated with sea-salt. The effect was very manifest; her improvement in all respects marked. The hæmorrhage disappeared, and she went until within a fortnight of her calculated time for accouchement. She gave birth to a living daughter, weighing five pounds.

Hæmorrhage during Labor.—Mrs. D. was taken with profuse hæmorrhage upon the first signs of labor, at 2 o'clock, A. M., on August 13. I was summoned immediately. Initial pains of labor occurred at moderately long intervals. Os uteri was very slightly opened, and a small portion of the margin of the placenta found over the os uteri. Perfect quietness was observed, and ice administered in small, but repeated portions; an enema of cold water was administered, which produced an abundant discharge of fæces. The tonic contraction of the uterus was unusually well maintained, and the presenting part (vertex) remained applied to the placenta. The first stage of labor was tardy, the os uteri opening slowly. When it became sufficiently dilated and soft, the membranes were ruptured, and delivery occurred at $2\frac{1}{2}$ o'clock, P. M. The child, a girl, was dead. The mother convalesced without difficulty.

Hæmorrhage after Birth of Child.—Cases need not be multiplied. Practical procedures are more worthy of consideration. As hæmorrhage under these circumstances always depends upon partial separation of the placenta, and will be arrested only when the separation of the mass becomes complete, it has been invariably a rule to effect the separation and delivery of the secundines without delay whenever flooding occurs.

An appreciation of the proper agency, by which the separation of the placenta is effected, is necessary to the adoption of the most direct means to excite that power when it is not brought into action opportunely or with sufficient vigor to detach the mass.

It is *not* the alternate or expulsive contractions of the uterus that effect the separation of the placenta.

The agent which detaches the placenta from the uterine surface is the tonic contraction of the uterus. This contraction, when fully exerted, separates and casts down the placenta upon the os uteri, whence it may readily be delivered. Frictions upon the abdomen over the uterus, alternated with compression of the uterus through the abdominal walls, will almost invariably induce the tonic contraction. Where the abdominal walls are much relaxed it will be found exceedingly serviceable to embrace the fundus, as much as possible, in the hand, formed into a cup shape, and thus to exert compression, following the fundus as the contraction of the body of the uterus draws it downward. Maintaining the hand in this position for a few minutes, will generally insure permanency of this contraction.

It must be an ever-remembered principle, not to use a tampon in any shape or form after the fœtus has been extruded from the uterus.

Hæmorrhage after Birth of Child, with Hour-glass Contraction of Uterus.—Hour-glass contraction of the uterus confining the placenta has occurred in five cases. The same general circumstances attended all the cases, and all were relieved by the same procedure.

Mrs. M. was confined at 10 o'clock, A. M., in an easy first labor; uterus well contracted on after-birth; after a short interval she complained of agonizing pain in the uterus, accompanied by a profuse hæmorrhage. The womb was found elongated, and examination discovered a firm hour-glass contraction, confining the placenta at the fundus. The hæmorrhage was continuous and profuse until the hand was introduced, the contraction overcome, and the placenta withdrawn. The flow ceased immediately as the contracting uterus followed upon the retiring placenta. No trouble was experienced in her convalescence. The large loss of blood did not delay the appearance of the milk.

Hæmorrhage after Expulsion of the Placenta.—The absence of feebleness of the tonic contraction of the uterus must be regarded as a fundamental condition for the occurrence of this hæmorrhage. I believe this to be true in every instance. I am aware that Dr. Gooch, in his "account of some of the most important diseases peculiar to women," has a chapter on "a peculiar form of hæmorrhage from the uterus," in which he thinks he disproves the universal applicability of the principle, that the absence of tonic contraction is the fundamental cause of hæmorrhage after the expulsion of the placenta. A very careful study of his cases will show the contrary of his view to be the correct one. A very able review of this chapter in Dr. Gooch's work may be found in the *American Journal of Medical Sciences*, Vol. viii., p. 419, from the pen of the late Professor Dewees. Professor Michaelis, of Kiel, has advocated views much like those of Gooch, but the most careful study I have been able to give to the cases of hæmorrhage in my own experience, has impressed my mind with the truth of the assertion, that in all hæmorrhages after expulsion of the placenta, (excluding, of course, cases of polypus, carcinoma, &c.,) the tonic contraction of the uterus is not perfectly or equally exerted.

It will frequently be found that the presence of clots in the uterus interferes with the healthful play of its actions, and that hæmorrhage of a profuse and painful character attends upon this condition. When this obtains, it will almost always be found that there is contraction of the internal orifice of the cervix uteri, offering obstruction to the escape of coagula, and causing them to plug the uterine orifice. This causes a false estimate of the amount of hæmorrhage by the external drain.

The following cases will illustrate the points. It is a subject of great importance, but the limits of a report prevent elaboration.

Mrs. K. was taken in her third labor about $12\frac{1}{2}$ o'clock on the morning of February 19. She had spent the evening with her brother's family, near her residence, and returned home about 11 o'clock. She retired and dozed At $12\frac{1}{4}$ o'clock she awoke with the pain of labor, and her husband immediately dressed and started for her accoucheur. He had scarcely left the house before the child was born. I, living immediately opposite, was instantly summoned, and, in not more than twenty minutes, was at her bedside. I discovered that the secundines had been delivered immediately after the birth of the child, and that tonic contraction of the uterus had utterly failed. She was almost pulseless, with a surface cold as marble, and able to articulate only in the feeblest whisper. An immense quantity of blood had been lost, and was still issuing freely. Supposing that no clots obstructed the cervix, I at once instituted brisk frictions over the uterus, with occasional graspings of the hand, while an attendant was instructed to prepare and administer a cordial. The uterus commenced promptly to contract, and in a few minutes had effected sufficient compression of the sinuses to stanch the flow. Constant vigilance was exercised over the uterus, to secure a continued contraction. When her accoucheur arrived, the hæmorrhage had been entirely arrested. This lady suffered the ordinary consequences of such great loss of blood, but otherwise convalesced well under the charge of her experienced physician. The child, although it had remained attached to the placenta for some time after the expulsion of that mass, did not appear to suffer from any loss of blood.

Mrs. R. was delivered at 10 o'clock, P. M., after an easy, but not rapid labor. The expulsion of the placenta followed in good time, and the tonic contraction of the uterus depressed the organ to its proper position. All things were promising well. After a short time she was observed to gape and become blanched, complaining of great pain in the uterus, and nausea. The hand upon the abdomen immediately recognized an irregularly contracted uterus; one portion seeming hard, while another was evidently relaxed. Friction upon the abdomen procured hardening of the relaxed portion, and the discharge of some coagula, but the intense pain was not mitigated. The hand was at once introduced into the uterus, and discovered coagula confined in a segment of the organ. These were removed, and immediately the uterus contracted equably, the agonizing pain disappeared, and the hæmorrhage was arrested. Nothing occurred to interrupt a favorable convalescence.

I may be allowed, without multiplying cases, to add, that none who were attacked by flooding died, with the exception of a case of placenta previa, which will be referred to under another head.

6. *Placenta Previa.*—The one thousand cases furnished three examples of placenta previa. An examination of reported statistics shows a great difference in the average number of placental presentations, as will be apparent from the following table:

Name of Reporter.	Residence.	Total number of Cases.	Number of Placenta previa Cases.	Per cent. of Placenta previa Cases.
Dr. Van Bibber*	Baltimore, Maryland	1787	7	.39†
Dr. Metcalf †	Mendon, Massachusetts	1768	4	.22†
Dr. Bliss ‡	New York	820	3	.36†
Dr. Pleasants §	Philadelphia	395	2	.50†
Dr. Storer ‖	Boston	440	1	.22†
Dr. Pierson ¶	Illinois	279	2	.70†
Dr. Kemp	Baltimore	1000	3	.3

A brief history of the fatal case of placenta previa may not be uninteresting. Mrs. M., in her thirteenth labor, was the subject of this case. I am indebted to her intelligent physician for a history of the case, prior to my being called to his assistance. There had been occasional hæmorrhage for a fortnight before she fell in labor. This was at no time very profuse, but the aggregate loss of blood had enfeebled her considerably. Labor commenced on the 6th of March, and was attended by great hæmorrhage. The ordinary means for suppressing hæmorrhage were instituted, and the vagina very compactly plugged. Her exhaustion became extreme. I saw her, with her physician, on the morning of March 7th. She was greatly depressed. Blood was escaping from the vagina sufficiently to show that the hæmorrhage had not been arrested by the tampon, but had saturated it most thoroughly.

* Transactions of the Medical and Chirurgical Faculty, 1855.
† Massachusetts Medical Society, seventy-fifth Anniversary.
‡ American Journal of Medical Sciences, N. S., vol. xiv.
§   "   "   "   "   "   "   xv.
‖   "   "   "   "   "   "   xx.
¶   "   "   "   "   "   "   xxxiv.

The tampon was removed. Examination detected the placenta in a great degree separated, and lying at the cervix. Hæmorrhage was still persistent. The placenta was entirely detached from the uterus, and withdrawn. The hæmorrhage instantly ceased. The head descended, and was promptly delivered. Tonic contraction of the uterus was well maintained. Appropriate restoratives were employed, and in several hours I took my leave. I had been called only to meet the crisis, and did not see her after my departure. I was subsequently informed that after repeated attempts at rallying, her powers of life gradually succumbed, and she died on the fourth day after her delivery.

The fact that hæmorrhage ceases upon the entire separation of the placenta when uterine atony is not present, is, I presume, no longer a matter of dispute. Since the cases of Simpson, Radford, and others, have been published, and the attention of accoucheurs has been directed to this specific point, many examples have occurred to confirm the accuracy of the fact; and a very important principle of practice grows out of these observations. A case has occurred in our own experience, (to be mentioned under another head,) where the first child and its placenta (in a twin case) were delivered for more than seven hours before the birth of the second. No hæmorrhage occurred after the expulsion of the first placenta. Dr. Metcalf mentions (in his address before the Massachusetts Medical Society) three cases in which "the placenta was thrown off with the last pains before the expulsion of the child; and in neither case did any hæmorrhage follow the birth." A case is recorded in *American Journal*, new series, vol. vi., p. 518, where both placentas in a twin labor were expelled after the first child, and no hæmorrhage ensued, although several hours elapsed before the delivery of the second child. In the same journal, vol. xviii., p. 122, is the history of a case of gastrotomy, in which the placenta was found lying unattached and without any hæmorrhage. In the same journal, vol. xi., p. 243, a case of arm presentation is narrated, in which the doctor, upon his arrival, found the placenta between the mother's thighs, entirely expelled, without subsequent hæmorrhage. The child was delivered by version, and the mother, who is represented as being faint and weak, had a successful recovery. The journals furnish an abundance of cases illustrative of the principle, that, with these two conditions obtaining, viz., a complete separation of the placenta from the uterine wall, and the presence of decided tonic contraction of the uterus, there will be no hæmorrhage. This introduces an important modification into the treatment of some cases of placenta previa, and affords a means of escape for the mother which was not acted upon before. I regard the discovery of the fact, and the construction of a judicious mode of practice so well calculated to enhance the probabilities of maternal life amid the perils of such cases, as constituting an era in obstetric medicine. I am not to be understood as regarding the separation of the placenta as the rule of proceeding in cases of placenta previa, but I am to be understood as believing that there are cases in which this procedure will save the mother, while the adoption of any other plan will be to forfeit the life of both mother and child.

7. *Liquor Amnii discharged long before Labor.*—Several cases occurred where the membranes broke and occasioned a stillicidium for a longer or shorter time before the invasion of labor. As there was special interest connected with one of these cases, it may be profitable to detail it.

Mrs. G was taken ill with typhoid fever on May 5th, being then advanced about six months in pregnancy. Her attack proved to be one of very unusual severity, and of protracted duration, evincing those profound vital lesions that invest the disease with its intensity and danger. On the 2nd of June, (the 28th day of her disease,) whilst prostrated extremely by her sickness, I was alarmed by the intelligence that a copious discharge of fluid from the uterus had occurred. It was beyond question indicative of a rupture of the fœtal membranes, and escape of the amniotic liquor. There was no indication of uterine pain, although it could scarcely be hoped that miscarriage would be prevented. The water drained off steadily, and in abundance. On the next day, the 3d of June, uterine pain was manifested with considerable severity and regularity, threatening the expulsion of the fœtus at no remote period, and thereby diminishing fearfully the hopes of the patient's recovery. This supervention of pain, and the mental anxiety occasioned by the critical circumstances of her case, tended to produce a display of nervous phenomena which aggravated those incident to the fever. The agent relied upon to suppress the uterine throes, and to restrain the high exaltation of the nervous system, was the Acetated Tincture of Opium, given in such varying proportions, with Spts. Ætheris Nitrici, as the necessities of the case appeared to require. The anodyne was varied in dose from five to twenty drops, and repeated at such intervals as would not induce absolute narcotism. Fortunately, the lady tolerated the medicine well. The contest, however, was not of short duration. The pain continued both day and night, despite the restraint of the anodyne, but evidently kept in abeyance by it, and it was not until the seventh day after its incursion that it was finally arrested. During this time the waters continued discharging. Rejoiced at the suspension of pain, I was still grieved to discover that the drain of water continued after the pain had been arrested, because I could not hope that my patient would ultimately escape miscarriage. Two days after the suspension of labor-pains, the water diminished sensibly in quantity, and finally ceased to flow. Hope for the lady brightened. Amendment of her general state soon became apparent, and she convalesced favorably until she recovered her usual degree of health.

She subsequently continued remarkably well, and gained greatly in flesh. She fell in labor on the 17th August, (two months and fifteen days from the rupture of the membranes.) The labor, which was her sixth, progressed most favorably, and she gave birth to a large, fat boy. I had looked forward to this accouchement with much anxiety and interest. Nothing dangerous attended the labor, but it was very remarkable that *there was only a trace of liquor amnii discoverable at any time during the labor*.

8. *Suspension of Labor-pains.*—It is a remarkable fact that sometimes, during the progress of actual labor, the pains will become suspended, and will remain so for a time varying from several hours to many days. Frequent examples have occurred among these 1,000 cases. This arrest of pain is not attributable to mental emotion or to physical exhaustion, since it occurs in labors which are natural in all respects, and in persons whose strength is not at all exhausted. The cause of this character of suspension is as yet, I presume, unascertained.

Mrs. H. fell in labor with her first child on August 19th, 1837, at 8 o'clock, A. M., in charge of Mrs. Hallar, an old and experienced midwife. The labor advanced regularly; by 12 o'clock considerable dilatation of the os uteri had been effected, and the waters protruded the membranes. A sharp expulsive pain ruptured the sac, and a quantity of the fluid escaped. The alternate contractions of the uterus instantly ceased, while the tonic contraction was exerted so decidedly as to maintain an unusual degree of firmness in the uterine walls. In all other respects the lady was well, and suffered in no way from this interruption. The midwife waited patiently from hour to hour for the return of pain, but abstained from any interference, inasmuch as the lady was, in no respect, suffering. At 8 o'clock, P. M., I was called, as some restlessness and fever made their appearance. There was no return of pain. Urine had not been voided for some hours, and the bowels were confined. The lady was able to evacuate the bladder voluntarily, which afforded her considerable relief. I abstracted about 12 oz. of blood from the arm, and ordered an aperient draught. At 5 o'clock on the next morning (20th) pain returned, and effected the delivery very propitiously at 10 o'clock, A. M.

Mrs. H in her first labor was taken with pains about 10 o'clock on the evening of Sept. 11, 1841, which continued with regularity and dilating effect upon the os uteri until about 5 o'clock next morning. Now, everything gave promise of a speedy delivery. The os had opened considerably, and permitted the waters to gather. At this time the pain suddenly ceased, unaccompanied by any indications of lesion. I waited patiently until after breakfast for the return of pain, but the uterus remained quiet. The lady suffered in no way that would justify interference, and I left, for the purpose of commencing my daily visitations. Returning repeatedly during the day, I found affairs in *statu quo*. So they continued until about 11½ o'clock in the night of the 13th, at which time pains returned, having been absent for 66½ hours, without any attendant evil. The pains continued active, and effected delivery in about 7½ hours after their recommencement.

Mrs. W., aged 43 years, in her tenth labor, was taken with pain on the night of 13th September, 1843, and summoned me about midnight. Her pains were active, and the soft, dilatable os uteri promising to offer no serious resistance to the passage of the foetus, we congratulated ourselves on the prospect of a happy ~~relapse~~ *Release* from the care and anxiety of a protracted watching. But, as Burns says,

> " The best laid schemes of mice and men
> Gang aft aglee."

We were doomed to disappointment, for, while we were expecting the membranes to rupture with every contraction, and had ideally seen the subsequent rotation, extension, and escape of the stranger's head, the uterus suddenly became quiescent. Under the circumstances, I supposed the truce could last but a few minutes. But no pains returned, and after several hours waiting, the fears of the lady and her friends becoming excited, they became clamorous that something should be done. It was apparent, from the lady's comfortable state, that no vital or organic lesion had crippled the uterine powers. I bethought me, too, that now might be illustrated the truth,

> " That when nae real ills perplex them,
> They make enow themsels to vex them;
> And ay the less they hae to start them,
> In like proportion, less will hurt them."

14

So I said, somewhat abruptly, "Well, if you insist upon my doing something, I have made up my mind to do the best thing that I can for her." "Do, doctor, do," was uttered by several anxious friends in concert. "But what are you going to do, doctor?" inquired the patient. I replied, "Why, madam, I am going home, as there is not the slightest risk to you in your present condition, and there can be no certainty when the pains will return." The matter took a pleasant turn for the present, and the lady, reassured by my communication, became entirely composed. One day passed; two days passed, and yet no pains returned. Friends heard of the singular circumstance, and "came to learn how it was." Wonderful accounts were given to the family of ladies who had gone undelivered for years, and the horror of thus carrying a child was graphically portrayed to the anxious lady. She was sustained, however, by her confidence in the truth of my assurances. But as day after day passed, and afforded no indication of returning labor, the number and the clamor of "friends" increased; divers consultations, (to which I consented, and the lady objected,) and every variety of obstetric operation were pertinaciously urged by the visiting friends. The most saucy of them felt at liberty to suggest, authoritatively, to me, their own thoughts upon my duty, and the dictates of an upright conscience, and imagined that I,

"Maun stan', wi' aspect humble,
An' hear it a', an' fear, an' tremble."

These folks were dealt with properly; but despite the outside clatter, the uterus remained at rest. I was assured that the child was living, and that "all was right" with the patient. She no longer confined herself to her chamber. Nine days elapsed from the suspension of pain until its return. On the morning of the 22nd of September, at 1 o'clock, I was sent for, and a very easy labor produced a plump, hearty girl, at 3½ o'clock, A. M., being only about two and a half hours from the onset of pain.

9. *Convulsions.*—The one thousand deliveries gave six cases of convulsions, two additional instances of cerebral congestion, which would, but for prompt relief, have resulted in convulsion or apoplexy, and one case terminating in apoplectic coma and death. Of these six cases of convulsion, two occurred before labor, and four during labor. Of the cases of cerebral congestion, one occurred during labor, and one subsequent to it. The apoplexy occurred after labor. Of the convulsions before labor, one was with a sixth pregnancy, and one with a fourth. The four cases occurring during labor were all in first pregnancies.

The cerebral congestion in labor was in a second pregnancy, and the case after confinement was a fourth labor.

All the children were head presentations. Four of the children were delivered by the forceps; the rest by the natural action of the uterus.

Of the mothers, one died; and of the children, one was lost.

Mrs. C. was confined for the sixth time on the 25th of July, 1843. She was of full habit, but accustomed to a considerable amount of exercise. On the 28th of June, nearly a month before labor, she complained of cerebral symptoms, which were relieved by a free venesection and an active cathartic, followed by a carefully restricted regimen. On the 16th of July, (nine days before labor,) she was seized with convulsions of an epileptic character, without the least premonition. She was again bled largely and purged, without an entire removal of the convulsions. The use of tartar-emetic in one-quarter grain doses, administered with a view not to its emetic action, but to its sedative influence over the nervous and sanguiferous systems, exerted a prompt effect in their subdual, and she did well until she fell in labor, on the 25th. During the dilatation of the os uteri, she was seized with a violent convulsion. She was again bled largely, and I was preparing to deliver her with forceps, when the uterus exerted itself powerfully, and I discovered the child ready to emerge from the vulva. The mother had one convulsion after the child was born. She continued subject for seven years to occasional returns of convulsions, when her habit became plethoric or her bowels constipated; but she never had an attack in a subsequent labor. She was treated by V. S. when indicated, and gently but steadily continued purgation and counter-irritation to the spine after each attack. For a number of years she has been entirely free from convulsion.

Mrs. T. was seized, on the morning of June 19, with spasm of the stomach and great dyspnœa, produced by offending ingesta eaten the night before. Her physician not being at home when called, I was sent for, and prescribed. Informed that she was daily expecting to be confined, I was careful in the selection of means for her relief. As soon as an aperient had acted freely upon her bowels, her pain and dyspnœa were greatly relieved. I was called late in the afternoon to see her in connection with her accoucheur, and found her in a strong convulsion. The os uteri was dilating under the influence of steady pain. The patient was bled, and delivered by forceps. The child was living. The mother continued insensible, and never rallied. It was a first labor.

Mrs. V., in her first labor, six days after the case above narrated. During the dilatation of the os uteri she was seized with a violent convulsion of unmistakably hysteric character. Pulse exceedingly rapid. A teaspoonful of Spts. Ætheris Sulph. Comp., and forty drops of laudanum, were administered, and the child delivered with forceps. The child was alive. There was no return of convulsion after the delivery.

Mrs. W's first labor commenced after midnight on the morning of August 26th. The lady was very stout in person, had lived freely, and taken very little exercise. Her bowels were confined. Castor oil was administered immediately after my reaching the case, which operated freely in four hours. As the pain became more active, she complained of headache, which was mitigated by local applications and quiet. There was no unusual activity of circulation. The womb dilated slowly, and she was suddenly seized with insensibility, followed quickly by convulsion. Immediately I bled her to a large amount, and her consciousness returned with the subsidence of the convulsion. Labor progressed slowly. About one and a half hours after the subsidence of the convulsion, a slight twitching of the face was observed, which proved the immediate precursor of another violent convulsion. During its continuance the capillaries of the head were intensely engorged. I bled her again largely, and she again recovered her consciousness. The oil had produced several large evacuations. I put her immediately upon the use of tartar-emetic, in sedative doses. The pains continued steady, but the uterus yielded slowly. The antimony appeared effective in subduing excitement, but nervous twitchings again coming on, and the soft parts permitting, I delivered her with forceps about 1 o'clock, P. M. The child was dead. The lady's convalescence was tedious, but ultimately her recovery was complete. Sixteen months after the last labor she was confined again; but having used proper regimen during the pregnancy, her accouchement was, in every respect, most happy.

Cerebral Congestion.—Mrs. R., second labor. I was summoned at 2 o'clock, A. M., of Sept. 5th. Pains very regular; os slightly dilated, but firm. Waters undischarged. About 3 o'clock she complained of headache, with intervals of ease; face slightly flushed and warm; pulse but little hurried, and not hard. Evaporating applications were made to forehead. Shortly after 4 o'clock she complained of her head feeling very large, and remarked that my size appeared to be greatly increased. Her head was hot and pulse fuller, with considerable firmness. I immediately bled her, until the sense of enlargement of the head was removed, and my figure resumed its natural size. After this there was no further threatening, and she was safely delivered at 7 o'clock, A. M.

Mrs. W. was safely delivered in a fourth labor on 25th November. She did well until feverishness attended the early secretion of milk. She complained of her chamber being too dark, and, at her bidding, the nurse arranged the window-blinds to admit more light. This answered as only a temporary benefit. Her sight being impaired, she directed a light to be procured. As she made no complaint of indisposition or pain, there was no special anxiety created. A large and handsome painting hung over the mantle, immediately in her full view. Her inability to discern the prominent points in the picture caused another light to be brought, and in a short time a third one was added. I was now sent for. I found her head hot, and eyes projecting; the pulse was very firm, but not full; the cervical vessels distended. She was perfectly rational, and complained of merely a fullness in her head. I directed the nurse to procure a wide basin. I made a large orifice in a vein of the arm, and the blood flowed in a full, rapid stream. I desired her to look at the picture over the mantle, and describe any apparent improvement in vision. After the blood had flowed to the amount of perhaps 10 ounces, she discovered points in the painting which were invisible before. I allowed the blood to flow, regardless of quantity, until she declared herself able to perceive the minute portions of the picture as distinctly as she could do in health. A slight tendency to syncope followed; she was afterwards purged actively. No further embarrassment to her recovery was experienced.

Mrs. H. was delivered at 5 A. M., February 12th, after an easy labor. Her habit was full, and her bowels had been torpid, although they were acted upon before the completion of labor. She did well until at my visit on the evening of the 13th, (about 36 hours after delivery,) when I discovered increased circulation and some headache. She made no special complaint. As a matter of safety, I directed the exhibition of a brisk, active purgative, and instructed the nurse to summon me if any necessity required it. I was called after dawn of day next morning, (14th,) and found her perfectly comatose. I received the following history: The lady declined taking the purgative, and the nurse acquiesced, without informing me of the lady's refusal. Nothing occurred to create apprehension, and at an early hour the family retired. The nurse awoke several times during the night, and remarked the apparently quiet and profound slumber of the lady. About day dawn she found it impossible to arouse the patient,

2

and then a messenger was dispatched for me. The coma was perfect, and, notwithstanding our efforts, the lady remained entirely unconscious, and died early on the next morning.

10. *Puerperal Fever.*—Puerperal fever occurred in six of the patients, but as one of the cases had puerperal metritis in three successive labors under my care, the whole number of cases would be *eight.* I need not enlarge upon this subject further than to detail a few cases, and comment upon the general plan of treatment.

Mrs. S. was the subject of the three successive attacks of metritis under my care. She was attended in her first labor by one of the most experienced accoucheurs in this city, but suffered a severe attack. Her second, third, and fourth labors occurred under my management, and although past experience induced great care in each successive pregnancy and labor, the disease could not be averted. In the last instance, it occurred on the eighth day after delivery. They all required active antiphlogistic measures, and all the attacks, happily, were subdued.

Mrs. B., delivered in second labor on 14th January, 1842. She suffered with severe abdominal tenderness and pain for three or four weeks before confinement. Bowels were distended, with flatus. After a restless night, she was taken early in the morning of 13th with irregular uterine pain. I saw her at 11 o'clock, a. m.; advised dry, warm applications to abdomen, and a dose of castor oil and laudanum. When it operated, it produced considerable tenesmus, and brought off one fœtid evacuation. In the evening pains had increased; examination discovered a head presentation; os uteri a little expanded, but quite soft. Much flatus in bowels. Administered a dose of calcined magnesia, which produced three watery stools, without amendment of pain.

At 12 o'clock at night the pain had made no progress of fœtus, and an enema of 60 drops of laudanum was administered. Os uteri a little more patulous.

8 o'clock, a. m.—Patient had some rest after the enema. Pains now are severe in sensation, but have no propelling effect on child. Os uteri quite dilatable. Vagina and perineum well relaxed; mucosity abundant. Head barely engaged in upper strait. A delay of one hour produced no improvement. Feebleness of pain was the evident cause of delay. The patient worn by her pains. Waters discharged. Administered 12 grains of ergot. Its action was apparent in five minutes, and the child was born in fifteen minutes from the adminis-

tration of the ergot. Uterus contracted well, and expelled secundines in forty minutes.

6 o'clock, P. M.—There have been few after-pains. Patient comfortable.

15th, 9 o'clock, A. M.—Complains of pain in uterus, with much flatulency of bowels. Ordered warm fomentations to abdomen.

6, P. M.—Just recovering from a chill. Pain diffused over abdomen, which is greatly distended. Some mental incoherence. Bowels not moved for forty-eight hours. Ordered a full dose of ol. ricini; continued fomentations.

9, P. M.—Oil acted once, and gave considerable relief; bowels less puffed; stool lumpy and fœtid; mind wanders occasionally; pulse 110; skin warm, and slightly moist; any motion produces pain; uterine globe very evident in hypogastrium, and sensitive to pressure. Lochia free. Prescribed calomel, camphor, and pulvis antimonialis, to be repeated every three hours. Black drops x, to be given *pro re nata*.

16th, 10, A. M.—One fœtid passage this morning. Had short slumbers during the night. Mind in a passively wandering condition. Lochia very moderate; abdominal pain reduced. Pulse 100. Prescribed 25 drops of black drop immediately, and repeat 15 every 1½ hour until sleep is induced.

7, P. M.—Has slept several hours altogether to-day. One nap of about 1½ hour's duration. Bowels distended; mind still unsettled; lochia scanty; pulse 89; skin nearly natural; no stool since morning. Ordered enema. As she has had but one dose (gtt xxv.) of black drop to-day, the nurse was directed to administer 30 drops after the enema operated.

It is needless to pursue the history further. The free use of black drop (short of narcotism) was continued, with occasional means to allay the intestinal flatus, until the 21st, at which time medicines were suspended, and her convalescence was confirmed.

The fatal case of puerperal fever may be briefly alluded to.

Mrs. P. was confined June 4, 1840, with her ninth child. Was under the care of a midwife. The patient had been very costive, and the midwife allowed the labor to go on with an impacted rectum. She suffered from flatulent pain and unusually rigid soft parts. When I saw her, I directed the bowels to be emptied by means of enema, and a dose of castor oil to be administered. After the clearing of the bowels, the labor was still delayed by unyielding soft parts; she was bled ℥xvj. Relaxation presently followed, and the child was safely born. I was not requested to see her again until some seventy-two hours after labor, when I found a well-developed case of puerperal peritonitis. The midwife had allowed her animal broths for nourishment, and directed her efforts mainly "to keep her strength up." The abdomen was now greatly distended, and exquisitely tender, with watery dejections from bowels. Pulse 120. On the 9th she vomited greatly, throwing up matter resembling finely-powdered charcoal. The case was badly nursed; her medicine was given with great irregularity, and she died on the 10th.

One case of puerperal fever occurred after a labor with twins, and, but for its being an isolated one, might be worth detailing. The point of interest is, that I had just returned from visiting a case of malignant erysipelas, when I was summoned to the labor. I had been called in consultation to visit a young lady nine miles from the city, ill with malignant erysipelas, and on my return to the city encountered a violent rain-storm, which completely soaked my gloves and thoroughly washed my hands. This, in addition to the washing given them before starting, would be presumed to have removed every infection of erysipelas. Upon reaching home, I found the message to the case of labor. This lady had a violent attack of the fever. After its appearance, I was careful to avoid contact with any of the secretions, and although five patients were confined quite shortly after this one, no other case of the fever occurred.

In regard to the treatment of the fever I may remark, that no one of the cases was bled after the appearance of the fever. They were purged early with calomel, and treated with liberal doses of opium, varied in form to meet any peculiarity of idiosyncrasy, and all, except the neglected case, recovered. The same general idea of treatment has been found equally beneficial in cases which I have seen in consultation.

11. *Engorgement of Cervix occurring during Labor.*—Mrs. H. was in her second labor on July 12th, 1837. The labor progressed slowly, both from inefficient pain and from an unusual indisposition in the os uteri to yield. The rigidity was not remarkable, but it remained at a certain degree of dilatation for several hours. The cervix was discovered finally to be hardening, and this condition increased to a degree of great engorgement and firmness, which effectually resisted any dilatation. A large venesection overcame the engorgement, and labor advanced to a successful termination for both mother and child.

12. *Impacted Rectum.*—It would seem almost impossible that an impacted rectum could obscure the character of a labor, and create a doubt in the mind of an experienced obstetrician. Nevertheless, on

the 26th of January, 1839, I was called in assistance to a very judicious and experienced practitioner, whose diagnosis was exceedingly embarrassed by what proved to be the superior portion of the rectum impacted with fæces. It presented the appearance of an arm of a twin descending with the head of the advancing child, and, at the then stage of labor, was well calculated to deceive. The patient having insisted (which was untrue) that her bowels had been moved several times freely, in the beginning of labor, gave still more occasion for deception. A very careful examination gave a solution finally, and the cause of difficulty was removed by aperients, after which the progress of the labor was rapid.

13. *Birth in Articulo Mortis of Mother.*—Mrs. M. in her third labor, child born on 4th of December, 1840. In the preceding October, I was called to attend her in an attack of dyspnœa, induced, without doubt, by long-continued torpor of the bowels. It was, however, relieved in four or five days by a persistence in aperients. She had suffered greatly from constipation during the entire pregnancy. In this attack her pulse was very small, frequent, and quick, and her expression of face indicated great organic suffering. Her relief was complete, and I saw no more of her until the 30th of November, when I was again called. At this time, I found her with indomitable vomiting, which commenced two days before. Her bowels had not been evacuated for a week, and the case presented unmistakable symptoms of volvulus. No appearance of any hernia could be detected. Pulse very small, and so rapid as not to be counted; fingers livid; respiration not greatly disturbed. On the 1st of December, a shriveling or wilting of the skin, as in the collapse of cholera, came on, without abundant sweating. On the evening of 4th December, she was dying. My mind was exercised about her child. Should it be removed by the Cesarean section immediately upon the death of the mother? I sat by her, anxiously watching. Laying my hand upon the abdomen, I discovered that the uterus was in action, and a vaginal examination detected the child progressing towards delivery. The action of the uterus was but little remitting, and the child was slowly but steadily advanced until it emerged from the vulva. The mother was in articulo, and survived but a short time. The child was dead.

14. *Frequent Special Presentations.*—Mrs. L. has had six labors; three were breech presentations.

Mrs. N. has had three labors; two were breech.

Mrs. B. has had four labors; two were breech.

15. *Frequent Twin Labors.*—Mrs. P. has had twins three times.

Mrs. K. has had twins three times.

Mrs. H. has had four labors; the third and fourth were twins.

16. *Mortality to Mothers.*—The total mortality to mothers in tho one thousand cases was as follows:

One from placenta previa.

One from apoplexy, occurring about forty hours after delivery.

One from puerperal fever.

II.—Pertaining to the Child.

1. *Months of Birth.*

January.	February.	March.	April.	May.	June.	July.	August.	September.	October.	November.	December.	Total.
92	73	72	65	70	90	88	88	83	100	82	97	1,000

Nearly half a century ago, Villermé, of Paris, in an essay inquiring into the distribution, by months, of human conceptions and births, found his statistics lead to the conclusion that fewer conceptions occur in the warm months of July, August, and September, than in any other three months of the year; and consequently, that the months of April, May, and June furnish fewer births than any other three months. The result in the above table corresponds nearly with this conclusion—March, April, and May offering the fewest births.

2. *Presentation.*

Whole No. of Cases.	Head.	Face.	Face to Pubis.	Breech.	Feet.	Knees.	Arm.	Shoulder.
912	865	2	13	26	2	1	2	1

Proportion of Special Presentations in Whole Number of Cases.

Presentations.	Cephalic Extremity.	Pelvic Extremity.	Arm.	Shoulder.
In 100.............	97	3	$\frac{2}{6}$	$\frac{1}{6}$

Analysis of Presentations with reference to Single or Twin Births.

	Whole Number.	Head.	Face.	Face to Pubis.	Breech.	Feet.	Knees.	Arm.	Shoulder.
Single Births	878	847	2	11	16	1	..	1	..
Twin Births	34	18	....	2	10	1	1	1	1

Two of the breech cases in single births were miscarriages, and not viable. They are included in the Table of Presentations, but will be excluded from Tables of Mortality.

Proportion of SPECIAL PRESENTATIONS *to each Whole Number in Single and Twin Births.*

	Whole Number.	Cephalic Extremity.	Pelvic Extremity.	Arm.	Shoulder.
		in 100	in 100	in 100	in 100
Single Births.......	878	$98\frac{2}{3}$	2	$\frac{1}{9}$	....
Twin Births........	34	59	$35\frac{5}{17}$	$2\frac{16}{17}$	$2\frac{16}{17}$

MORTALITY *in the different Presentations in Single and in Twin Births.*

	SINGLE BIRTHS.				TWIN BIRTHS.			
	Whole No.	Deaths.		In 100.	Whole No.	Deaths.		In 100.
Head	847 }	10 }			18 }	1 }		
Face...	2 } 860	.. } 10	10	$1\frac{1}{9}$	.. } 20	.. } 1	1	5*
Face to Pubis ..	11 }	.. }			2 }	.. }		
Breech	14 }	3 }			10 }	1 }		
Feet	1 } 15	1 }	4	$20\frac{2}{3}$	1 } 12	.. }	1	$8\frac{1}{2}$
Knees	}	.. }			1 }	.. }		
Arm	 1	1		....	.. 1	1		..
Shoulder	....	..		....	.. 1	..		..

* I have doubts whether this child was dead when born. The circumstances of the case make me think that the woman would have concealed her delivery altogether, if it had been possible. She was alone when this child (the first of twins) was delivered, and, from appearances, I supposed it had been born alive, but died because the woman did not know how to take care of it. She asserted, however, that it did not cry or breathe after its birth. I could discover no marks of violence about it. See comments on case 148, under head of "Twins."

The three last preceding tables show:

1st. The great disproportion between the number of head presentations in single and in twin births, being in single cases 98 in 100, and in twins 59 in 100.

2d. The greatly preponderant number of presentations of the pelvic extremity in twin cases, being 35 in 100, while in single births it is 2 in 100.

3d. The excessive number of unnatural presentations in twin cases, being 2 in 34, while it is only 1 in 878 in single births.

4th. The diminished mortality in nates presentations in twin cases, being $8\frac{1}{3}$ in 100, while in single labors it is $26\frac{2}{3}$ in 100.

I thought it advisable and instructive to introduce, in this place, the general comparative tables of single and twin births; thus showing the facts at one view, rather than to reserve those leading facts until the subject of twins shall be considered. The specialties of twins will be treated in the appropriate place.

Proportion of Special Presentations in Single and Twin Births, under different Obstetricians. The fractions, with large numbers, are disregarded.

	Single Births.					Twin Births.				
	Whole No.	Cephalic Extremity.	Pelvic Extremity.	Arm.	Shoulder.	Whole No.	Cephalic Extremity.	Pelvic Extremity.	Arm.	Shoulder.
		in 100	in 100	in 100	in 100		in 100	in 100	in 100	in 100
Dr. Metcalf	1746	97	$1\frac{2}{3}$	$\frac{1}{1746}$	$\frac{1}{1746}$	22	68	32	....	....
Dr. Burwell	546	96	$3\frac{1}{84}$	....	$\frac{2}{78}$	20	70	30	....	....
Dr. Kemp	878	98	2	$\frac{1}{4}$	....	34	59	$35\frac{5}{17}$	$2\frac{4}{17}$	$2\frac{1}{17}$

I regret that so few *American* statistics of midwifery have been published. Those which time has allowed me to examine afford, from their omission of minutiæ, no data upon which to construct a table upon this point more extensive than the foregoing.

Face Presentations.—The two children who presented the face were born alive. In connection with the record of the first case, the following note was made in the register at the time: " In this case the violence and rapidity of the pains prevented its rectification." It stands as No. 401 in the register, and I was influenced then by the opinion that all such cases should be rectified if possible. I attempted the rectification, but promptly abandoned it, on account of the strength and frequency of the pains, which, it was apparent, would deliver the fœtus in good time. There was no excessive discoloration or sugillation of the face; and altogether it resulted as well as if it had been a vertex presentation.

In the second case I made no attempt to interfere.

Having received my obstetrical precepts from the teachings of that accomplished practitioner, the late Professor Dewees, I felt impelled to adopt his procedures in the difficulties experienced in my early professional life. His reverence for the authority of Baudelocque indelibly impressed on my memory the assertion of the latter, that "for them (face presentations) to be terminated without help, it is requisite that the head should be very small, and the mother's pelvis, at the same time, very large; otherwise they become very long and difficult, the children are born with the face tumefied and livid, and almost always deprived of life, or ready to lose it, on account of the engorgement of the brain." It was in my mind a fixed precept before I saw a case of face presentation, that in such a labor the position of the head *must be rectified if possible*, whenever the head and pelvis were of the ordinary dimensions. I was therefore ready, when, at half past 2 o'clock A. M., alone and far from help, I encountered my first face case, to rehearse my aphorism, and proceed to comply with its requirements. The head was not *very small*, neither was the pelvis *very large*, and I trembled for the result in case I failed to rectify the head. The severity and frequency of the pain (and I have no doubt my maladroitness assisted) prevented my succeeding. I saw the effect of the throes advance the head, and, in a sad desperation, I carefully watched its progress. The labor was soon ended; the child was living, and but little disfigured; and I learned a new lesson from observation.

I was induced to study this subject more extensively, and by the time my second case occurred I was prepared to meet it composedly, and let it make its own way into the world.

The mind of the profession has been divided as to the proper course to be pursued in face presentations. Until the latter part of the last century, the majority of obstetricians believed that it was *almost* impossible for these labors to be accomplished without assistance, and the discussion of the question with them was limited to the kind of assistance to be afforded.

Turning was at first considered as the only orthodox practice, and an attempt to afford relief by any other means became allowable only when turning was impracticable. So strong was this belief, that even Dr. Davis, of England, says, in his Elements of Op. Midwifery, "There can, in my opinion, be no doubt of the preferableness of turning to all other modes of treatment." When, more than one hundred years ago, Gifford published two cases of face presentation, delivered by the extractor, he appears to have felt it necessary to offer something like an apology to the profession for not practicing version; for he introduces the remark, that version is extremely difficult when the waters have been discharged, and the child is closely embraced by the uterus.

The history of the subject furnishes, from time to time, the opinions of those who entertained different views, and adopted a practice conformable to their convictions. Portal, La Motte, Deleurye, and others, had unequivocally asserted from observation, or published cases demonstrative of the fact, that face presentations do not necessarily require artificial assistance; but that, in the words of Portal, "in such cases no violence must be used, but nature be left to its own course; which done, there is no danger to either mother or child." Notwithstanding the expression "no danger," in Portal's opinion, the reports of cases left to nature show a somewhat increased mortality over vertex presentations.

Nothing tended to illuminate the subject so much as Boer's publication, in 1793, of eighty cases of face presentation, which occurred in the Vienna Lying-in Hospital. Of the eighty cases, but one was assisted, and there were three or four of the children born dead.

A careful study of the relation of the diameters of the child's head to the diameters of the pelvis during the transit of the fœtus, will show an adaptation almost as favorable as in vertex cases, and (except when the chin turns into the concavity of the sacrum) offering but little more embarrassment to its expulsion from the vulva. Let any one perform the mechanism of this labor on the obstetric fantom, and he will discover that the three diameters of the fœtal head to be regarded in face presentations, are the fronto-mental, the bi-malar, and the trachelo-bregmatic, which correspond respectively with the occipito-frontal, the bi-parietal, and the cervico-bregmatic in vertex presentations, and offer about the same measurements.

These *two* cases of presentation of the face, in one thousand deliveries, correspond very nearly with the general average as disclosed in United States statistics.

Face to Pubis.—I can give an analysis of only twelve cases in which the face was towards the pubis; and as there may be several points of interest in their detail, they are presented in tabular form.

Analysis of Cases presenting Face to Pubis.

Number of Case in Register.	Number of Labor.	Sex.	Weight.	Alive or Dead.	Single.	Twin.
195	4	B	7½	Alive.	Single.	....
216	5	B	10	do.	do.	....
259	4	B	7½	do.	do.	....
265	1	B	..	do.	....	1st Twin.
283	2	G	7	do.	do.	....
293	6	B	9	do.	do.	....
370	2	B	8½	do.	do.	....
382	5	G	9¾	do.	do.	....
459	5	B	8½	do.	do.	....
513	3	G	..	do.	do.	....
532	6	G	..	do.	do.	....
540	5	B	..	do.	....	2d Twin.

Cases 216 and 293 were in the same person, and 370 and 513 were also in the same person; in both instances, it will be perceived, the labors were consecutive.

It is a little remarkable that the first occurrence should be only at the 195th case; and although the different numbers are not widely separated, there was no case from 540 to 1,000. This may be possibly accounted for, in part, by the fact that somewhere about the time of the occurrence of the last case, I became interested in determining, by my own observations, the accuracy of the great Heidelberg professor's opinion, that at the commencement of labor the cases of the 5th position of vertex (Baudelocque) were much more numerous than the second. This led me to ascertain, as early as practicable, the precise points about the presenting part; and I find, in the column of the register for remarks, such comments as the following: "5th position naturally rotated into 1st;" "4th naturally converted into 2d;" "4th changed by hand to 2d," &c.

I am certain, however, that the number from 540 onward would have been much less than previously.

There was nothing specially interesting in any of the cases, except Nos. 216 and 370, in which the labor was considerably more tedious than I thought would have been in a vertex case.*

---

* It is a very important point not to confound the mechanism of labor in which the face is to the pubis, with the mechanism of labor in face presenta-

Presentation of the Shoulder.—This was the second child in a case of twins; the first child was a vertex presentation. It stands No. 148 on my register, and I sincerely regret that my notes on the case give nothing of the mode of the second delivery, except the remark, "Cephalic version was successful, and it was born as a head case." The child was saved. I have no accurate recollection of the manner in which it was accomplished, and will not venture any explanation.

Presentation of the Arm.—There were two cases of presentation of the arm; one a single birth, the other the second child of a twin labor. Both were delivered by version, and both were dead.

Presentation of the Pelvic Extremity.—As the cases of breech, knee, and foot presentations resolve themselves into the same condition towards the completion of delivery, they may properly be considered in one group.

The 1,000 cases of delivery furnished 29 cases of presentation of pelvic extremity, of which 26 were breech, 2 feet, 1 knees.

Two of the breech cases were abortions; and as they were consequently not viable, they will be excluded from tables in which mortality is calculated.

Analysis of Presentations of Pelvic Extremity.—Excluding the two breech abortions in single labors, in which the children were not viable, we have 27 cases remaining for analysis.

tions; nor to suppose that these two modifications of head presentations offer to the touch the same impression.

To one who observes carefully the exit of the head from the vulva, when the forehead is at the pubic symphysis, the extreme distention of the vagina and perineum affords just ground for fearing laceration of these soft parts. The cause most usually assigned for the increased risk of perineal rupture is, that the coaptation of the forehead to the arch of the pubis being less complete than that between the arch and the vertex in vertex cases, the head must in the former position press backward more strongly, and thus distend the perineum more extensively in order to escape at the vulva. But as, in this delivery, the vertex is born first, and turns posteriorly to allow the face to emerge, the forehead is very seldom brought under the arch until after the vertex has escaped. The forehead is behind rather than under the arch, and the diameter of the head which expands the vagina is that traversing the head from the back of the neck to the anterior fontanelle, the cervico-bregmatic; after the escape of the vertex, the fourchette and perineum are compelled to bear the strain of the whole power that is necessary to bring the forehead between the rami of the pubis, as it passes into the world.

Cases	No. of Labor.	Sex.	Presentation.	Alive.	Dead.	Single Labor.	Twin Labor.
1	12	......	Breech.	Alive.	....	Single.	....
2	3	Boy.	do.	....	Dead.	do.	....
3	3	Girl.	do.	do.	....	do.	....
4	..	Boy.	do.	....	do.	do.	....
5	2	Girl.	do.	do.	....	do.	....
6	7	Boy.	do.	do.	....	....	2d twin.
7	2	Boy.	do.	....	do.	do.	....
8	1	Boy.	do.	....	do.	....	2d do.
9	1	Boy.	Feet.	....	do.	do.	....
10	4	Girl.	Breech.	do.	....	do.	....
11	...	Boy.	Feet.	do.	....	....	2d do.
12	3	Girl.	Breech.	do.	....	do.	....
13	6	Girl.	Knees.	do.	....	....	2d do.
14	1	Boy.	Breech.	do.	....	do.	....
15	5	Boy.	do.	do.	....	....	1st do.
16	1	Girl.	do.	do.	....	do.	....
17	4 {	Boy.	do.	do.	....	....	1st do.
18		Girl.	do.	do.	....	....	2d do.
19	....	Girl.	do.	do.	....	....	2d do.
20	1	Boy.	do.	do.	....	....	2d do.
21	4	Boy.	do.	do.	....	do.	....
22	3	Boy.	do.	do.	....	....	1st do.
23	....	Boy.	do.	do.	....	....	2d do.
24	....	Boy.	do.	do.	....	do.	....
25	....	....	do.	do.	....	do.	....
26	4	Boy.	do.	do.	....	....	2d do.
27	6	Girl.	do.	do.	....	do.	....

The table, condensed, gives the following points:

Whole No. of Cases.	Breech.	Feet.	Knees.	Males.	Females.	Alive.	Dead.	Single Child.	Twin Child.
27	24	2	1	16*	9*	22	5	15	12

The delivery of the cases (excepting Nos. 7 and 16) was accomplished without instrumental aid

Cases No. 2 and 3 were the respective lady's second breech labor.

Cases 12, 21, 27 occurred in the same lady.

Case No. 4 was delivered of the child by a midwife.

Case No. 9 was not delivered under my superintendence.

The child in Case 7 was very large, and, not presenting a due correspondence of diameters with the diameters of the pelvis, it became literally jammed into the passages, and I was called to the assistance of the physician in charge. After much exertion, the delivery was

* The sex of two of the children was not noted.

secured with entire safety to the mother, but with the loss of the child.

Case No. 16 was a primipara. The only interference in her case was the use of a ribbon in the groin to facilitate the descent. The danger to the child begins especially with the delivery of the umbilicus, and becomes greatest when the head enters the pelvic straits. A few practical aphorisms treasured in the memory become eminently useful to the young obstetrician in his early experience in these cases.

Frequency of Presentation of the Pelvic Extremity.

	Whole No. of Cases.	Breech.	Feet.	Knees.	Total.	In 100.
Dr. Van Bibber	4,192	61	20	..	81	1.93
" Bliss	771	16	8	..	24	3.11
" Storer	440	5	3		8	1.81
" Pleasants	400	7	3	..	10	2.5
" Burwell	598	17	9	..	26	4.34
" Pierson	265	1	3	1	5	1.88
" Metcalf	1,768	18	13	3	34	1.35
Bellevue Hospital	1,348	27	20	..	47	3.48
Dr. Potter	247	3	9	..	12	4.85
" Warrington	332	8	..	.	8	2.40
" Kemp	912	26	2	1	29	3.17
Total	11,273				284	

The totals give an average of a little more than $2\frac{1}{2}$ presentations of the pelvic extremity in 100 deliveries.

An examination of the table reveals a great difference in the average of pelvic presentations as they are presented in the different statistics. I shall not attempt to form an opinion as to the cause of such discrepancies, believing that no fixed law determines these things, and that no practical good could result from such inquiry. It is interesting only as constituting a part of the facts which make up the entirety of obstetrical statistics. A far more interesting study is the mortality in breech cases, and the best means of procedure to lessen that mortality—or, in other words, to have our minds posted with a knowledge of what we are not to do, as well as with what it may be necessary for us to do in these cases.

I had designed to prepare and introduce, at this place, a table giving as full details as possible in reference to the ratio of mortality in presentations of the pelvic extremity of the fœtus, but upon examining the statistics I find that the reports are so meagre in details necessary for a useful table, that but little practical information could be gathered. I had designed also to analyze the facts of the table, and to deduce whatever of value in practice might appear in their results. I hoped to do this from the statistics which the practitioners of the United States have contributed to the journals, and thus arrive at the practical views which govern the obstetricians of our own country. I shall be glad to know that some abler hand may undertake this duty, and furnish this United States experience to the profession.

Mortality.—I can only comment on the mortality exhibited in my own table, and present such reflections as may appear apposite. It will be observed that in the last eighteen cases no child was lost. I have no doubt that the practical views which control the management of the delivery of breech cases have much to do with the fate of the child; and I regard it to be incumbent upon every one who undertakes to preside at a breech labor, to have in his mind a code of rules, embracing details, calculated to insure the most successful results to both mother and child.

I may, therefore, expect to be pardoned for giving a few of the points which I think should be regarded with much care in these cases. The books teach with distinctness their prominent and general circumstances, and enlarge sufficiently upon their indications and management. These cannot be even adverted to upon an occasion like the present.

The practical precepts which, in my judgment, should regulate the accoucheur's conduct in uncomplicated presentations of the pelvic extremity, are:

1st. The presentation of the nates can seldom be perfectly diagnosticated by the touch before the rupture of the amniotic membrane, because the presenting part generally remains high in the pelvis for a considerable time after the commencement of labor; and as the remoteness of the presenting part is not peculiar to the nates, *therefore,* in all such cases, *a careful examination must be made immediately after the discharge of the waters, to ascertain the precise characters and position of the presentation.*

2d. If the knees are presenting, they may rest upon one side of the pelvis and prop the breech upon the opposite side, so as neither to advance themselves, nor to allow the breech to traverse the pelvis; *therefore,* in knee presentations, when the knee is disposed to rest against the side of the pelvis, *if the uterus is abundantly dilated, push* up the whole of the presenting parts in the absence of pain, and bring down the feet; then leave the case to the natural powers.

3d. In breech and feet presentations, do not bring down the feet to expedite delivery. The evil effect of such ill-advised measure is experienced when the head comes to be delivered. There is high authority for bringing down the feet in breech cases, but the *weight* of authority and the teachings of experience are against the operation. The presumed necessity for any interference arose, at first, from the supposition that the pelvis did not afford room for the child to pass in this doubled condition, and hence cephalic version was the remedy proposed. This not succeeding, it was first proposed and practiced by Ambrose Paré, to bring down the feet, in order to lessen the bulk and to facilitate the delivery. Several later writers have advocated the practice. *But it is unquestionably a bad practice.* Ramsbotham tells us that William Hunter was once an advocate for this procedure; but afterwards he adopted the opposite views, and was accustomed to acknowledge in his lectures, "that when he used to extract the legs before the breech, he lost almost every child; but when he changed his mode of practice, and let the breech pass double, and did not allow the legs to escape until after the knees were born, he was much more fortunate in saving the children."

4th. In nates presentations the arms are generally in close apposition to the sides, with the forearms flexed and crossed on the breast; and the labor is finished with more facility if the arms continue in this position, than if, from any cause, the elbows become arrested in their descent, and the arms become unfolded and extended on the sides of the head as it enters the pelvis. *Therefore do not draw upon the breech to hasten the descent of the child, but let it be accommodated slowly to the passages, lest the diameters of the child may not be accurately adapted to the diameters of the pelvis, and the elbows may be arrested and the arms unfolded.*

5th. If it be important to aid in the descent of the breech, recollect that the fœtus, by coinciding with the axis of the upper strait, will descend with the anterior hip in advance of the posterior, until it reaches the floor of the pelvis. At this point rotation occurs, and, as now the axis of the lower strait is to be traversed, the posterior hip advances, while the anterior one remains nearly stationary at the pubic arch; *therefore, in giving aid to the descent of the breech before it fully occupies the cavity of the pelvis, the greater amount of traction must be made on the anterior groin; but after the breech occupies the cavity, traction must be made on the posterior groin.* ALL EFFORTS OF THIS KIND MUST

BE MADE IN ASSISTANCE OF THE PAINS, AND, IN THE ABSENCE OF MOST URGENT NECESSITY, SHOULD NEVER BE EMPLOYED WHEN THE PAIN IS OFF.

6th. When the breech is born, the temptation is very great to draw upon it and help the labor along; FORBEAR.

7th. When the umbilicus is born, the cord is apt to become tense, and evil may result; *therefore the cord should be drawn down to a sufficient extent to prevent any tension during the delivery of the superior parts of the fœtus.*

8th. After the delivery of the umbilicus, and the relief of the cord, ascertain the position of the arms. If they do not descend with the breast, by the natural powers, they will be placed by the sides of the head in its transit through the pelvis, and may retard delivery. *It is well, therefore, to bring them down at this stage. The posterior arm should be brought down first; the power should be applied, as nearly as possible, at the elbow, and the arm brought over the face and breast.*

9th As the shoulders are about to emerge from the vulva, the head is engaging in the pelvis. As the descent of the head will be facile or delayed according to the extent of its flexion in bringing the chin close upon the breast, and as the pressure of the uterine contraction is the means by which this flexion is secured, *therefore do not hurry the shoulders through the outlet, lest, by partially withdrawing the head from the uterine power, you not only prevent its flexion, but may cause such a degree of extension as to embarrass the further descent of the head.*

10th. When the shoulders are fully born, the head has engaged in the pelvis, and has descended, perhaps, entirely beyond the influence of the uterus; its further expulsion by uterine contraction cannot be hoped for; *therefore, in this state, exhort the patient to exert her powers in bearing down, so that the abdominal and pelvic muscles may detrude the head.*

11th. There is great danger to the child if the head is long delayed in the pelvic passages, for the cord will be compressed between it and the pelvis; thereby the fœtal circulation will be arrested; and, as there is more or less separation of the placenta and compression of the uterine sinuses occasioned by the tonic contraction of the organ closing its cavity after the receding child, the fœtus will fail to receive due supplies of oxygenated blood, and may fall a victim to asphyxia or cerebral congestion; *therefore endeavor to afford the child an opportunity to respire, and thus to decarbonize its own blood. To accomplish this, elevate the child's body towards the abdomen of the mother, and pass the hand (not a few fingers) along the posterior wall of the vagina until the*

*points of the fingers fully pass the mouth; then press back the soft parts,
so as to afford access for air to the child's mouth.*

12th. *Never pull upon the body to deliver the head, for thereby the
head is likely to be extended, and the delivery made more difficult;* but if
there arise a necessity for interference to disengage the head from the
pelvis, *adopt the procedures taught in the books for promoting a greater
flexion of the head, and a closer approximation of the chin to the breast;*
then extractive force exerted upon the shoulders may be made success-
fully.

3. *Mortality in Individual Instances.*—Of the 11 deaths *in head
presentations,* (10 single and 1 twin,)

Three were dead before the incursion of labor.

Two were in cases of placenta previa.

One in a case of contracted pelvis, with tedious labor, delivered
finally by the forceps.

One in a narrow pelvis. In this case the labor was protracted.
In the last preceding pregnancy, I delivered the lady of a living child
with forceps, after having suffered the labor to linger for some hours;
but the case having been criticised by an authority whose experience
was supposed to have made him a competent judge, the present case
was allowed to progress with strict reference to the injunctions laid
down by leading English authors. The mother's condition was regarded as the indication for interference. Her state required no
assistance, and the natural powers were left to finish the labor. In
her subsequent pregnancy, the same condition of labor prevailed, but
as soon as the soft parts fully warranted interference, I applied the
forceps, and delivered a living child.

One was in a case of convulsions.

Of the *breech cases* I have no special notes. One was the second
child of a twin birth.

Of the *arm cases,* two in number, both were dead-born.

The first occurred March 29, 1835. Whilst the lady was dining,
the membranes ruptured without any premonition, and a large amount
of water escaped. The patient lived more than three miles from my
residence. I was immediately summoned. When I reached the case
labor was active, and examination discovered an arm presenting,
doubled on itself at the elbow. I immediately informed the family of
the difficulty to be apprehended, and, being in my professional noviti-
ate, desired consultation. The gentleman who came to my assistance,
diagnosticating a *knee,* insisted, against my remonstrance, in bringing
down the *foot.* This he attempted, but it proved to be the *hand.* I pro-

posed to subdue the powerful action of the uterus by venesection and anodynes, and to deliver by version. He dissented, but proposed to remove the arm at the shoulder, &c. This led to the calling of additional assistance. Uterine pains were abated by a very large bleeding, with large doses of opium, and a very large child was delivered by version. In three weeks the woman walked to the city and rode home in a wagon without springs, but sustained no appreciable injury.

The other arm case was the second child in a twin labor, delivered by version.

4. *Time of Birth.*—In 495 children, the precise time of birth is noted. These give 249 born between six o'clock A. M. and six o'clock P. M., and 246 born between six P. M. and six A. M.

In 526 children, (including the foregoing,) the births marked A. M. or P. M., counting midnight and meridian as the extremes, were as follows: 301 A. M., 221 P. M., 4 M.

5. *Sex.*—In 788 children noted, there were 427 boys and 361 girls.

6. *Weight.*—Fractions are disregarded.

Pounds	3	4	5	6	7	8	9	10	11	12
Children	1	1	4	12	36	47	48	9	2	..

Making the average weight of 160 children to be about 8 pounds.

7. *Position of Presentation Changing.*—The views of Naegele took the professional world somewhat by surprise, when his published opinions were found to controvert the order of frequency in which presentations of the head were presumed to occur. I was induced to examine my cases more carefully, and as early as the condition of the os uteri would permit, and I became satisfied that many of the cases delivered in the second position of the head (vertex to right acetabulum) were in the commencement presenting with the vertex at the right sacro-iliac junction, (4th of Baudelocque.) Nay, more than this occurs; for I have, with the finger on the presentation, followed the head in its change from the 5th position to the 1st, and have received it at the birth as though it had been an original first.

The mobility of the head, while it is above the upper strait, is so great, that the voluntary movements of the fœtus frequently sweep the extremities of the cranial diameters over almost the entire semi-circumferences of the basin. This may be easily verified by retaining the finger in contact with the head in the intervals of pain. It appears, then, very plain that, at whatever point of the circumference of the strait the vertex may be when a pain occurs that will force it to engage in the strait, it will maintain that position until it descends to the point where rotation is to be effected. Under these circumstances, the vertex may engage at either extremity of the oblique diameters, if it be found there when the pains thrust it down into the strait. But if the child be small, or the pelvis be large, the position will continue to the end of labor; otherwise, the vertex will be rotated forward on its side of the maternal pelvis, and be delivered at the pubis.

While the fact of change of position is undeniable, my observations do not bear out Naegele's assertion, that the 4th presentation of the vertex is more frequent than the 2nd, at the beginning of labor.

This subject presents many points of interest to those who delight in recognizing the wisdom and the goodness of God, as manifested in all his creations, and the wonderful adaptedness of all his designs to subserve the best interests of his creatures. We here see structures arranged apparently for a certain end, and those ends accomplished almost universally with great precision, by means which we cannot fully understand.

The fact that the fœtus almost always presents in a manner calculated to enable the natural powers to effect its delivery, is, in itself, an incontestible evidence of a wise Designer and Creator. The remarkable tendency which malpositions of the head manifest, to be reduced to some natural presentation, and thereby render the delivery more conformable to the mechanism of the more favorable; the wonderful propensity of the vertex, when it presents posteriorly, to offer at the pubis in the last stage of labor, thus securing the most happy result from an inauspicious beginning; the law or force which determines the rotation of the vertex into the hollow of the sacrum, and brings the chin to the pubis in face presentations, in which, if the vertex be brought to the arch, a life is almost necessarily lost:—these demonstrate a most wonderful, wise, and good Creator. Moreover, in every variety of nates presentation, if the case be not injudiciously interfered with, the same incomprehensible power has ordained the rotation of the face to the sacral excavation as the most constant mechanism, and the one by which the probabilities of the infant's life are greatly enhanced.

These phenomena cannot fail to excite in the reflecting observer emotions of admiration and most profound reverence.

The mysteries connected with the inception of vitality in the ovum, and the remarkable arrangements for the perfection of that life with the organic development of the fœtus, are but a part of the series of displays of infinite power, wisdom, and goodness in this portion of creation. How true are the words of the gifted but unfortunate Boyse:

> " E'en the weak embryo, ere to life it breaks,
> From his high power its slender texture takes;
> While in his book the various parts enroll'd,
> Increasing, own eternal Wisdom's mould."

8. *Twins*—The 1,000 deliveries gave 19 cases of twin labor.

Two of the labors were abortions, with boys, before the children were viable, and a note of the sexes only was made. Nothing occurred different from the circumstances of a single abortion, except that in one case there was considerably more blood lost than usually attends an ordinary case.

These two cases will properly be excluded from any calculation of mortality, but will be used in the comparison of sexes.

Analysis of Twins.

No. in Register.	No. of Labor.	Presentation.		Sex.		Weight.		Interval between Children.	Alive or Dead.	
57	1	Head.	Head.	B.	B.				A.	A.
108	6	....	....	B.	B.					
136	..	....	....	B.	B.					
148	1	Head.	Shoulder.	G.	G.			11½ hours.	*D.	A.
226	7	Head.	Breech.	B.	B.	6¼	6½	25 minutes.	A.	A.
265	1	Face to Pubis.	Breech.	B.	B.			....	A.	D.
333	2	Head.	Head.	B.	G.	5½	6½	....	A.	A.
415	4	Head.	Feet.	B.	B.			....	A.	A.
463	6	Head.	Knees.	G.	G.	6½	6½	45 minutes.	A.	A.
540	5	Breech.	Face to Pubis.	B.	B.			20 minutes.	A.	A.
574		Head.	Head.	B.	G.			1 hour.	A.	A.
590	1	Head.	Arm.	G.	G.			1½ hour.	A.	D.
600	4	Head.	Breech.	B.	G.			20 minutes.	A.	A.
609	2	Head.	Head.	B.	G.			15 minutes.	A.	A.
635	..	Head.	Breech.	G.	G.			15 minutes.	A.	A.
666	1	Head.	Breech.	G.	B.			....	A.	A.
730	3	Breech.	Head.	B.	G.			....	A.	A.
794	1	Head.	Breech.	B.	B.			....	A.	A.
878	4	Head.	Breech.	B.	B.			....	A.	A.

* See note to Table of " Mortality in the different Presentations in Single and in Twin Births," under the head of " Presentations."

Nos. 108 and 136 were abortions—the children not viable.

Nos. 108 and 226 occurred in the same person. The latter number was her third twin labor.

No. 136 was the lady's third twin labor.

No. 600 was the lady's second twin labor.

Nos. 730 and 878 were consecutive labors in the same person.

The nineteen labors were afforded by seventeen individuals, of whom,

13 produced twins for the first time.

2   "   "   "   second time.

2   "   "   "   third time.

Preceding Table Condensed.

FIRST CHILD.						SECOND CHILD.					
Presentation.	Total.	Alive.	Dead.	Male.	Female.	Presentation.	Total.	Alive.	Dead.	Male.	Female.
Head	15	14	*1	10	5	Head	6	6		2	4
Breech	2	2		2		Breech	7	6	1	5	2
						Feet	1	1			1
						Knees	1	1			1
						Shoulder	1	1			1
						Arm	1		1		1
Abortion				2		Abortion				2	

The presentation of the shoulder was converted into one of the vertex by cephalic version, but as, at the time of its occurrence, I made no extended note of the manner of its being accomplished, I think it improper to do more than state the mere fact that it was done.

This case (148) is interesting, however, in other particulars which were fully noted at the time. The woman was alone when her first child was born, at 1 o'clock, A. M. She says she had great hæmorrhage after the birth of the first child until something pushed down into the upper part of the vagina, at which time the bleeding ceased. I saw her first at 10 o'clock, A. M., nine hours after the birth of the child. There was no hæmorrhage now. The placenta was partly in the vagina and partly in the uterus. I removed it; discovered another child in utero. She had very trifling pains. I waited until 12 M. The membranes of the second child were still entire. The indisposition of the uterus to act with decision caused me not to interfere hitherto. At 12 M. I gave her fifteen grains of ergot, which acted

* See note to the Table of " Mortality in the different Presentations in Single and in Twin Births," under the head of "Presentations."

slowly, producing a moderate amount of pain. I ruptured the membranes and then promptly examined again, and detected the shoulder. This was rectified, and the head, brought to the strait, was delivered in a short time. The child was alive, but feeble.

A point of considerable interest is the length of time during which the placenta was detached, before the birth of the second child. About eleven hours must have elapsed between the separation of the first placenta and the birth of the second child, allowing that the sensation of something pushing into the vagina marked the time of the casting off. The occurrence of circumstances like these has greatly modified the opinions formerly entertained of the danger to the second child, as well as of the hazard to the mother from hæmorrhage. We might here advert to the manner of vascular connection between the uterus and placenta; the source of hæmorrhage, when a portion of the placenta is separate from the uterine wall; and the probable reason why hæmorrhage is generally suspended by the total detachment of that mass. This would involve a review of the many interesting experiments and dissections which have been made upon the human subject, as well as upon inferior animals, and would require a discussion of the proper application of these facts in directing the practical treatment of cases not infrequently occurring in the experience of accouchenrs. However interesting and profitable the consideration and attentive study of these cases may be, we are forbidden, by the occasion, to enlarge upon them. We will dare, however, to urge the members of this faculty to give great diligence to the study of the later literature of this subject, as affording much that is interesting in fact, and that conduces to the highest good of those who intrust their lives and their health to the knowledge and judgment of the medical practitioner.

The presentation of the arm (Case 590) occurred with a second child, and was delivered by version.

Case 226 was the lady's third pregnancy. The two children appear to have had originally separate placentæ; but in the progress of gestation they became united to a sufficient extent to allow the coalescing and fusing of the two chorions. The delivery showed that each child had his funis and amnios distinct, whilst a common chorion enveloped them both. By the laws, generally acknowledged as operative in the production of monsters, we must suppose that if, in a case like this, the amniotic sacs had had their contiguous portions removed so as to allow contact between the germinal membranes of the children, and the position of the children had been similar, the result would, most robably, have been a fusion of the children and the birth of a monter. But as the presentations were respectively head and breech, no monster would have resulted. The case is suggestive of many interesting reflections, in which, however, we must not now indulge.

In Case 463 the two placentæ were fused for a considerable extent of their circumference, and came away united in this manner.

In Case 540 there was one large placenta, but a distinct funis for each child.

In Case 609 the birth of the first child was perfectly ordinary. In ten minutes after its delivery a powerful and continuous pain delivered the second child enveloped in its membranes, with one large placenta common to the two children.

The following table demonstrates a varying proportion of twin cases, as they occur in different series of observations:

	Whole No. of Cases.	Twin Cases.		Authority.
Dr. Warrington...	354	3	1 in 118	Am. Journal Med. Soc. N. S.,Vols. 1, 3, 5.
" Burwell.....	588	10	1 in 59	" " " " 7
" Bliss	820	8	1 in 102	" " " " 14
" Pleasants	420	5	1 in 84	" " " " 15
" Storer	451	5	1 in 90	" " " " 20
" Pierson	274	5	1 in 55	" " " " 34
" Metcalf	1,786	11	1 in 162	Annual Address Mass. Med. Society, 1856.
Bellevue Hospital.	1,410	23	1 in 61	" " "
Dr. Potter.......	304	2	1 in 152	" " "
" Cock.........	533	15	1 in 36	" " "
" Van Bibber...	2,503	17	1 in 147	Med. & Chirurg. Faculty of Md., 1855.
" Kemp......	1,000	19	1 in 53	
Totals	10,443	123		

This table gives, by considering the totals, a general average of one twin labor in about 85 cases.

I have heretofore cited only statistics furnished by practitioners in the United States, because I have been anxious to arrive at the result of *American* experience, as that which most concerns us, and should ever be a subject of much interest to those who estimate their country aright.

I contemplate, with gratification, the day when the published experience of physicians in the United States will be sufficiently full to furnish a mass of American facts which shall be a rich contribution to the literature of obstetrics, and when the principles and laws deduced from these facts shall be considered necessary aids in determining great questions of science. Let our practitioners but carefully record their cases, and publish the results of a sufficiently extensive series of observations, and the United States will command her honorable rank in the scientific councils of the world.

The comparative frequency of twin labors in different countries may be seen by connecting the totals of the last table with a table of European statistics given by Churchill.

	United States.	British.	French.	German.
Whole Number, ...	10,443	161,042	36.570	251,386
Twin Labors, ...	123	2,477	332	2,967
1 in	85	69	110	84

Sex of Twins.—It may not be uninteresting to refer to the sexes of twins, as appear by the following table:

No. of Cases.	Both Male.	Both Female.	Male and Female.	Total Males.	Total Females.
19	9	4	6	24	14
in 100	$47\frac{7}{19}$	$21\frac{1}{19}$	$31\frac{11}{19}$	$63\frac{3}{19}$	$36\frac{16}{19}$

This series shows a different result from other published tables, in the following particulars:

1st. In the number of "Both Males" being greater than "Both Females."

2d. In the number of "Male and Female" being greater than "Both Females."

3d. In the number of "Total Males" being greater than "Total Females."

The following tables give United States and English numbers:

Author.	No. of Twin Cases.	Both Males.	Both Females.	Male and Female.	Country.
Dr. Metcalf's Table.......	38	11	17	10	U. States.
Dr. Kemp's Cases	19	9	4	6	Do.
	57	20	21	16	
Dr. Churchill's Table....	457	131	145	181	England.
Dr. Ramsbotham's Cases..	536	171	183	182	Do.
	993	302	328	363	

9. *Children Diseased.*—One of the children gave incontestible evidence of disease arising from syphilis in the father.

In one case the child died about the $4\frac{1}{2}$ month of gestation; the only assignable cause being syphilis in the mother. The child was retained until the full period, and the entire ovum was then born in one mass; the placenta and membranes enveloping the child unbroken.

Another case, illustrating the communication of small-pox to the foetus in utero, is sufficiently interesting to justify a narration of the circumstances.

A lady was seized with a chill, followed by high fever and great headache. During the evening labor came on. After her delivery, symptoms, anomalous in the parturient, persisted, unattended by any indications of metritis, peritonitis, or any apparent phlegmasia. The symptoms resembled those of a severe malarious fever, yet no plausible occasion of such attack could be assigned. On the third day an eruption bestudded her surface, attended by a decline in her arterial excitement. I diagnosticated variola, and immediately vaccinated the infant. On the seventh day after birth variola appeared upon the infant, and pursued its ordinary course. The child survived the disease, and recovered perfectly. The circumstances evidently show the infection of small-pox in the infant while it was in utero.

One child died of idiopathic umbilical hæmorrhage.

10. *Deformed.*—There were eight cases of deformity, and one case of absence of the anus and lower part of rectum. Of these,

One was a case of double hare-lip and double cleft palate.

Two were cases of single hare-lip and cleft palate.

Two were cases of club-foot. These were interesting, and, being worthy of note, will be described more at length presently.

One was a case of tumor on occiput. This will be described presently.

In one child the two first fingers of left hand were adherent to the second joint.

In one child (a breech presentation) the thighs were adherent to the anterior wall of the abdomen until within a very short distance from the knee. The integument of the abdomen was continued around each leg throughout the entire distance of the adhesion. One arm was adherent in like manner to the neck and face as far as the elbow, and the shoulder-joint of that arm was immovable after the attachment of the arm to the neck and head was severed. If the child had been a head presentation, it is very likely the thighs would have been torn from their adhesion to the abdomen in its delivery. It lived for some hours after its birth.

Club Feet.—The two cases were children of the same parents. A perfect child was produced at an intermediate birth. The first case was clubbed in both feet; one foot was an extreme degree of varus; the other foot was a less degree of the same variety. The second case was one of varus also, one foot only being distorted. The great practical interest of these cases consists in their both having been perfectly restored by the use of apparatus, without any operation. The plan of treatment was that detailed by Dr. Heber Chase, of Philadelphia, in the *American Journal of Medical Sciences*, New Series, Vol. I., p. 88; and also in the *Maryland Medical and Surgical Journal*, Vol. II., p. 181. I must not, on this occasion, detail the particular steps of treatment, but I will most earnestly endeavor to impress these cases upon your memory, that you may be prepared to adopt so successful and so simple a plan of cure, in any cases that may fall under your observation. The complete success in these cases proves the correctness of the principles which the apparatus is designed to carry out so completely.

Tumor on Occiput.—This case was in charge of a very intelligent gentleman, who had watched it for some hours, and when he felt embarrassed was, very properly, unwilling to institute any procedures without counsel. When I examined the case I discovered a round, firm body, closely resembling a child's head, but without fontanelles or sutures, occupying the cavity of the pelvis. Upon exploring it fully, it presented the same characteristics at every point of its surface, except a circular space about the size of a dime-piece. Pressure upon this spot detected a contained fluid. It was impossible to discover the part to which the tumor was attached, inasmuch as its size and extreme firmness prevented any examination beyond. The tumor was pierced at the soft spot, and the contents discharged. This afforded an opportunity to ascertain that the vertex was ready to engage in the upper strait. The finger was inserted into the rent in the tumor, and traction made by it upon the head, which promptly entered the pelvis and was born by a few pains. The tumor was covered by a prolongation of the integuments from the junction of the nucha and occiput; its walls were firmly cartilaginous, and its cavity evidently communicated with the cerebro-spinal canal.

Absence of Anus.—In this case an operation was performed to find the lower terminus of the bowel. Selecting a spot where we supposed the anus should be, a very careful exploration was made by Professor

Baxley, in the direction of the ordinary course of the rectum, until he had penetrated the distance of more than an inch, when a slight appearance of meconium announced that the bowel had been reached. The opening was delicately enlarged, and the operation was completed. For a day or two there were hopes of success, but an inflammation supervened internally, and the child died.

11. *Fœtus Retained from Early Months.*—Several cases occurred in which the fœtus perished in the early months of pregnancy, but was retained until the expiration of the ordinary term, and was delivered in a state of preservation, without any trace of putridity.

12. *Length of Funis.*—A number of cords was carefully measured, but as your time would be unprofitably consumed by lengthy remarks and comparisons, I may simply state that, of the cords measured, the shortest was 15 inches, and the longest 53½ inches in length.

13. *Intestinal Hæmorrhage of the Child.*—In this case profuse intestinal hæmorrhage occurred on the third day, causing extreme exhaustion of the child. It was promptly arrested by administering one-drop doses of tinct. ferri sesquichlor. suspended in a little mucilage, and repeated at intervals of two or three hours.

14. *Head firmly Ossified—Third Position of Baudelocque.*—This was the lady's second labor. *The almost entire obliteration of fontanelles and sutures greatly embarrassed the diagnosis of the presentation.* I saw the case at 10 o'clock, A. M. Pains were recurring at intervals of six and eight minutes. Os uteri slightly open; presenting part beyond reach of the finger. At 12 M., the os was more dilated, thick and soft, with small bag of waters. At 3½ P. M. the soft parts were well relaxed; os uteri well dilated. The waters were at this moment discharged by a pain. The head was found resting at the brim of the pelvis, but as I could perceive neither a fontanelle nor unequivocal suture, I was unable to determine the position of the head. The hand was now introduced into the vagina, when, by the contour of the head and the position of the ears, the vertex was found presenting at the pubis. The head was moved into the second vertex position, and strong uterine contractions having been provoked by the manipulation, the child descended rapidly, and, the pelvis being capacious, the delivery was accomplished in fifty minutes. When the head cleared the vulva, the vertex turned to the left thigh of mother, as in an original first position of vertex. The placenta followed in twenty-five minutes. The child was large, and the head remarkably ossified. The anterior fontanelle was almost entirely obliterated. The lady had gone a month beyond her expected delivery.

15. *Instrumental Labor.*—Instruments were resorted to twenty-eight times in the 1,000 cases, giving an average of $2\frac{4}{5}$ in 100, or 1 in $35\frac{5}{9}$, for the use of instruments.

In these cases the vectis was used three times, the forceps twenty-two times, and the perforator three times, giving an average employment of the vectis once in $333\frac{1}{3}$ cases; of forceps once in $45\frac{5}{11}$ cases; and of the perforator once in $333\frac{1}{3}$ cases.

The VECTIS was used in the three cases to effect a better coaptation of the head to the diameters of the pelvic canal.

In one case the PERFORATOR was employed to lessen the head, which was pitched in the iliac fossa. When I saw the case, (in consultation,) labor had been active for some hours, and the waters had been long discharged. The physician in charge had unsuccessfully endeavored to use the vectis and the forceps, but had not attempted version. The vagina was becoming hot and tender, and the child afforded no indications of being alive. Under these circumstances, the perforator was deemed the proper means for the accomplishing of the delivery, and it was effected readily in this way. The placenta was so firmly adherent as to require to be peeled from the uterine wall by the hand. In the other two cases, the promontory of the sacrum jutted so far into the upper strait as not to afford space for the passage of the unreduced head. Neither of the cases was a first labor. These cases occurred before the recent disenssion of the propriety of version as a substitute for the crotchet; and as no information was obtained bearing upon the basis of said disenssion, I can merely report them in this simple manner.

Analysis of Forceps Labors.

Number of Labor....	1	2	5	6	7	8	10	12	Not Designated.
Number of Cases........	13	2	1	1	1	1	1	1	1

The table is to be read thus: the forceps were used in 13 first labors; in 2 second labors; in 1 fifth labor, &c.

In four of the first labors, the forceps were used to deliver the fœtus on account of convulsions in the mother.

In the fifth labor case the pelvis was deformed to an extent sufficient to interfere with the delivery of the child. Seventeen months previously, I had attended the lady in her fourth labor, at which time her child was born alive by the natural powers. A deformity of the pelvis was observed at that time, but it was not sufficient to prevent, although it greatly retarded, delivery. But at the time of her fifth labor, the deformity had increased, and after waiting several hours for the unassisted pains to thrust down the child, I feared the consequences of a longer delay, and applied the forceps. The delay which I allowed was, however, too long for the safety of her soft parts, and I was grieved to see a urinary fistula as the consequence of that delay. I feel certain that the forceps had no agency in the production of the slough, and that I might possibly have saved the child and preserved the integrity of the vesico-vaginal septum, if I had used them an hour or two earlier in the labor.

The 6th, 7th, and 8th labor cases occurred in the same lady. The forceps were used in each case when the head was occupying the cavity of the pelvis. At this point in each labor, the pains became feeble and inefficient. The soft parts were perfectly prepared for delivery, and a longer waiting would have involved much anxiety and suffering for the patient.

The 10th and 12th labor cases happened in the same person. The pelvis was narrow, and unassisted delivery, with an ordinary child, would necessarily be very tedious. In the 10th labor, when the head descended to the straitened pass, it soon became apparent that much effort must be expended in forcing its way by the natural powers. The soft parts were well relaxed and lubricated, and I preferred the assistance of the forceps for present relief. The child was born alive, and well. Eighteen months after this, her 11th labor occurred. For reasons mentioned under the head of "Mortality in Individual Instances," this case (the 11th labor) was not assisted, and the child was born dead. In the 12th labor I had recourse to the forceps, and the child was born alive and strong.

The reasons for the use of the forceps in the 22 cases may be succinctly stated thus:

Four times on account of eclampsia.

Once on account of deformed pelvis.

Twice on account of narrow pelvis.

Fifteen times to assist the passage of the head through the pelvis, because of delay in the second stage of labor.

I pray you to bear with me in occupying a portion of your time by offering some comments on the table, and some reflections on the use of forceps in the deliveries.

With those who entertain the opinion that first labors are of all others generally the most illy adapted to any interference from the accoucheur, it may excite the spirit of criticism to be told that, of the 22 forceps cases, 13 were primiparæ. But why are first labors, more than others, supposed to offer difficulties and objections to the use of forceps, and why are they generally expected to be longer in duration than others? Is it because of the undue rigidity of the soft parts, and their indisposition to relax? This cause cannot be assigned with equal plausibility for first labors in all the different years embraced within the child-bearing period of women. The books assign this as a cause for tedious labor when it occurs in those who marry late in life. If this be true, those who marry soon after maturity should be (cæteris paribus) exempt. We know that in first labors, at all ages, the first stage is frequently protracted and exhausting, and often produces an enfeebled and irritable womb in the second stage, thereby causing the uterine contractions to be peculiarly painful, and at the same time ineffective. This, I apprehend, is attributable to the fact that the process of labor, when induced for the first time, awakens new influences and sympathies in the system, and in this, as in the majority of new actions in the organs, the parts, thus newly affected, do not promptly obey the reflex impressions communicated to them. But whatever may be the cause for this tardy softening, which gives character, in the judgment of so many, to a first labor, I may ask at once the question, But if relaxation has already occurred, wherein does a first labor differ in indications from any other labor? Why, under these circumstances, are not the same means of relief equally as applicable in a first as in any other labor?

The great difference of opinions, as to what constitutes a necessity for the use of forceps, has beclouded the question, and nothing but a patient criticising of those opinions, and a careful examination of the results of practice, can clear up the subject to any one's mind. The fœtal and maternal mortality which some have reported in forceps deliveries, and their grave comments and cautions, have tended to create an unjustifiable prejudice against the instruments, and have, doubtless, deterred many from carefully studying their indications and their powers. The ordinary manner of reporting statistics conveys the idea that the deaths were caused by the forceps; than which nothing is more unjust. Examine any series, and see how many of the cases would have been fatal even if the forceps had not been employed; aye, when the forceps were the means upon which the only hope of life was based. Charge the forceps with such death! As well charge one with the death of a drowning person whom he endeavors to rescue.

48

because he *could not* save the unfortunate. A false estimate has arisen from these statistics, and a fear of the forceps *per se* has been created.

Let any one examine the cases of those who are fearful of the forceps, and who permit the labor to linger for hours, in the hope of a natural delivery, or until symptoms of local lesion or vital exhaustion alarm them to a necessity for action, and he will read the history of many who most probably might have survived, if the forceps had been used before the incursion of such extreme circumstances. Can any practitioner believe with Ashwell, that the necessity for artificial assistance arises only when "the pains become weak, short, and inefficient, producing no effect on the head of the child, &c.; if the pulse, the countenance, and the general appearance of the woman are expressive of extreme debility and fatigue, a strong presumption is afforded that we have waited sufficiently long to unassisted nature; if, in addition to these symptoms, we have headache, mental inquietude, shivering and vomiting, a pulse of 120 or 130, furred tongue, a hot skin, great thirst, abdominal tenderness, heat and soreness in the vagina and os uteri, we feel assured our patient has approached to a state, from the evil consequences of which instrumental aid will alone deliver her?" If his practice conform to this doctrine, his record would indeed be a sad commentary upon the forceps as a means of saving life, or even abridging the unnecessary sufferings of a fellow-creature. It is not the forceps that makes the way for death, but it is the delay of the accoucheur, which has allowed the head to compress the soft parts at one point for hours, until inflammation is beginning in the maternal tissues, the exhausted uterus is in a state of atony, and the crippled vitality of the structures is unable longer to preserve their integrity.

Even Dr. Collins seems to have had unnecessary fears in the use of the forceps, for he says: "Generally speaking, so long as the pulse remains good, the bowels and bladder act well, the soft parts remain free from severe pressure, and uterine action continues, so as to cause the presenting part to descend ever so slowly, the patient having no pain in the abdomen on pressure, or local distress, the child at the same time being alive, I am satisfied no attempts should be made to deliver with instruments, and that he who does so wantonly exposes both mother and child to danger." "A prudent use of instruments, in the practice of midwifery, is of great importance; but the necessity alone of freeing our patient from impending or present danger, should induce us to resort to them." Is the amount of suffering endured by the patient during the hours that the presenting part is descending "ever so slowly," and the ultimate evil results which frequently happen, to have no weight in the mind of the accoucheur? Is it judicious to let the struggle go on for hours, simply because nature may be able finally to complete the delivery, when there is good reason to apprehend that the triumph of nature will be achieved at the expense of the future health and well-being of the mother?

There is truth in the opinion of Mr. James Wilson, of Glasgow, that "deficient or deranged uterine action is the chief cause of the difficulties and delays in parturition; and that for one case of protracted labor where the pelvis or the position of the head is in fault, there will be twenty occasioned by deficient or imperfect uterine action."

I remember distinctly my feelings when I first used the forceps on a living frame. It was a first labor, and, after a tedious and harassing first stage, the head had descended to the perineum, and the vertex was pretty fairly applied to the arch of the pubis, the perineum was relaxed abundantly, and the vagina was quite moist, but the pains did not urge the head onward to delivery. The patient was *impatient*, but I was firm in my purpose not to interfere, because I had read that the forceps was a very dangerous instrument, and that they should not be used until "the ear is within reach for six hours." I looked at my watch again and again, but never did time roll its wheels so slowly. I was satisfied that, if it were possible to deliver her by applying my hands upon the sides of the head and making traction, that the delivery would be productive of no harm. This I could not do. What, thought I at last, are forceps but artificial hands, and why not use *them*? I had carefully studied the application of the instrument, and resolved, in this case, to let circumstances, not hours, govern me. The parts concerned were fully prepared for delivery. I applied the forceps, and in a few minutes relieved the sufferer, with perfect safety to herself and child; and I appeal to any candid, unbiased mind to say, whether I did not a good and a perfectly justifiable deed.

We sometimes meet with cases in which the head is apparently ready to pass under the arch, but where it remains stationary, notwithstanding the womb continues to exert itself energetically. There is no malposition nor want of space, yet the strongest pains fail to effect its dislodgment. Cazeaux explains this difficulty by the head becoming so flexed as to destroy the leverage at the occipito-atlantoid articulation, and to allow the spine to be driven down upon the occiput, and thus to create the greatest possible flexion of the head, and

4

prevent the operation of the pains in the direction of the axis of the lower strait. In such cases, (and they occur frequently in first labors,) when all things are ready, I have no hesitation in affirming that the forceps should be used, the ear and six-hour law "to the contrary notwithstanding."

I had commenced to arrange materials for the construction of a table calculated to exhibit the results in forceps operations, so far as the forceps were justly chargeable with those results. I designed to exclude all children who were known to be dead before delivery, all who gave evidence at birth of having been some time dead, all delivered dead by the forceps under circumstances which would have inevitably destroyed them independently of the instruments, &c.; and by this means would have attempted to place the forceps (on the side of the prosecution) "*rectus in curia*." But the time for their full arrangement could not be spared from my daily duties, and the patience of attentive and kind friends has already been sufficiently tried. However inviting the field to me, the length already attained by this report admonishes me to pause.

I beg to add one more remark under this head. I seldom use anæsthetics, of late years, in my cases, and I carefully avoid them when about to perform any operation; for, in addition to many other cogent reasons which I might detail, I am impressed with the soundness of the views so pointedly uttered by Professor Meigs in his letter to Professor Simpson: "The best guide of the accoucheur is the reply of the patient to his interrogatory, 'Does it hurt you?' The patient's reply, 'Yes' or 'No,' is worth a thousand dogmas and precepts, as to planes and axes, and curves of Carus. I cannot, therefore, deem myself justifiable in casting away my safest and most trustworthy diagnosis, for the questionable equivalent of ten minutes' exemption from a pain, which, even in this case, is a physiological pain."

16. *Time between Birth of Child and Delivery of the Placenta.*—This subject will be disposed of in a few words. I can give no table of time, because it is an invariable rule with me (if nothing forbid) to effect the discharge of the placenta whenever the tonic contraction of the uterus is firmly established, and the after-birth thereby thrown upon the os uteri. In my earlier years I pursued a different plan, while I thought a tardy expulsion of the placenta secured a comparative exemption from severe after-pains.

And now, gentlemen, fellow-members of the Medical and Chirurgical Faculty of Maryland, I have attempted to fulfill a duty which your kindness induced you to intrust to me as the chairman of your committee. The matter has expanded far beyond my anticipation, and subjects which should have been fully discussed have been necessarily treated in a cursory manner. I have, however, done what time and circumstances would allow. I have dared to hope that this may be a contribution (however humble) to the mass of American facts which is accumulating by the industry and care of our American physicians. If you should deem some of the sentiments to have been uttered too didactically, I can only ascribe the manner to a want of familiarity with writing for the public eye or speaking to the public ear; and, with a sincere desire to learn, can say, "*Si quid noristi rectius istis, candidus imperti.*" I sincerely hope some abler hand may be devoted to the elaboration of these subjects, as with physicians it is emphatically true, that "we must live and learn."

"*Nemo enim ad cognitionem veritatis magis propinquat, quam qui intelligit, etiamsi multum proficiat, semper sibi superesse quod quærat.*"